with thanks to Megan
C.F.

Library of congress-in-Publication Data available

3 5 7 9 10 8 6 4 2

Published in 2002 by Sterling Publishing co., Inc.
387 Park Avenue South, New York, NY 10016
First published in Great Britain in 2002 by Gullane children's Books
Winchester House, 259-269 Old Marylebone Road, London NW1 5XJ
Text and illustrations © Charles Fuge 2002
Distributed in Canada by Sterling Publishing
c/o Canadian Manda Group, One Atlantic Avenue, Suite 105
Toronto, Ontario, Canada M6K 3E7

Sterling ISBN 1-4027-0137-3

I Know a Rhino

Charles Fuge

Sterling Publishing Co., Inc.
New York

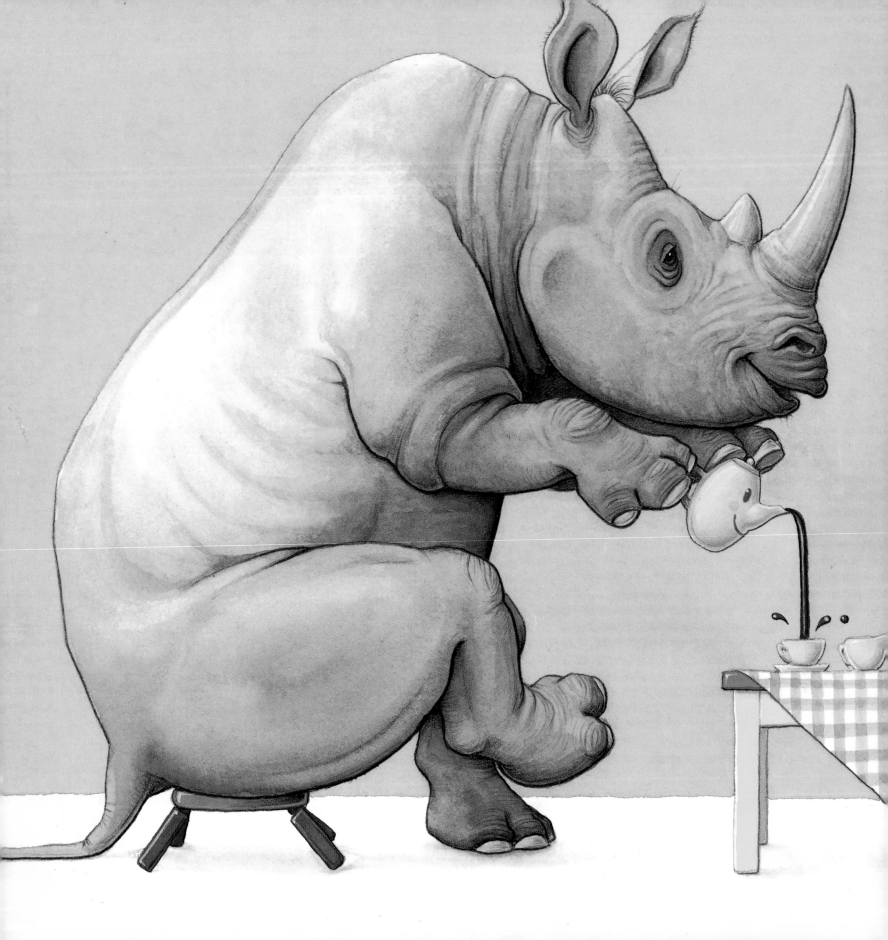

I know a **Rhino.**
We like to take tea.
I have **two** sugars
and Rhino has

three.

I know a **Pig** and we play in the **dirt**.

We always have **mud fights** but no one gets hurt.

I know an **Ape** and we keep in **good shape,** singing **pop** songs and dancing along to a **tape.**

I know a **Hippo** and when she's not busy, We spin **round** and **round** until we get **dizzy**.

I know a **Dragon**.
He's scaly and bold.
I look after him
when he's
got a bad
COLD.

I know a **Giraffe** and
we laugh and
we laugh,
Blowing hundreds
of **bubbles**
when we take
a bath.

I know a **Bear** and when it is sunny, we go for a picnic with brown bread and **honey.**

I know a **Leopard** who loves to get dressed. In a **suit, tie,** and **top hat,** he's simply the **best.**

These are my friends.
I know them, you see.

I know them quite well . . .

MAY 1 1 2010